KNIFE

for Mars

KNIFE

Russell Helms

SJ

first edition

ISBN: 978-1-943661-34-3

sij books
booksbysij@gmail.com

The Bulgarian Orthographic Reform of 1945

Terence stood on his head in the corner. He used to make soup for the homeless. Amelia lay in bed, bleeding. She wasn't sure from where. She worked at the Green Stamp store near the bridge. Rain blew in the open window.

"Help me," said Terence.

"I'm pregnant," said Amelia. "The sheet needs washing."

Under the bed, Terence saw a steak knife, a sock, and balls of pink fuzz.

"I'm bleeding. The bullet hole is weeping," said Amelia.

"I thought the bullet hole was okay," said Terence. He felt a warmth gathering in his beard.

Amelia scanned his smooth legs and swollen face. She saw the bottle of vanilla extract on the floor. It was easier to steal than whiskey. They were broke. He had colon cancer. She missed her piano lessons.

The weight of Terence's body drove his face into the floor, twisting his ropy neck. Foam seethed between his loose teeth.

Amelia figured her fistula was how Terence had gotten her pregnant. But the redheaded woman, Gina, next door, had shot her husband, Andrei, right about then. The bullet had blown through his cods, burst through the plaster in Amelia's tiny bedroom, nicked the music stand on the beat-up piano, pierced Amelia's secret place, and zipped into Scarlet's apartment next door. Scarlet worked nights and had a heart condition. The paper probably mentioned it.

Amelia inched her way to the side of the bed, a glow rising in her chest. She pulled Terence's tattered underpants over his ankles and tilted the little bottle right in there. She was going to be a mother after all, and hopefully Terence was the father. Their neighbor Andrei was a conniving commie linguist with coke-bottle glasses. He deserved to have his cods shot off. She peeled off her fake mustache. Maybe things would work out after all.

The Piano Tuner

Amelia answered the door and retreated inside as if the sunlight were dangerous. The man standing there reminded her of Andrei. What she needed was a friend. She was lonely. He followed her into a pale yellow living room where she tripped over a small, beat-up piano. The bench sagged.

A long-necked boy tethered to the piano's leg looked up at the man and began to cry without noise. An icy splash of water fell from beneath the woman's skirt onto the floor. The ice water soothed the fistula and kept it from getting angry. The boy retreated to the outer reach of his tether and grimaced.

Andrei placed his canvas tool pouch on the small green sofa. He smelled like vanilla extract. The woman dropped a towel onto the water and asked Andrei if he was blind yet. He was not, he said, but he knew a piano tuner who was. He talked like a teenage girl. He asked her how long it had been since the piano was last tuned. She looked at the tentative boy who said it had been thirteen years.

Andrei waited for Amelia to tidy her mess before lifting the piano top. He peered inside and pulled out an old manuscript. He folded the yellowed papers and stuffed them into his pocket. He plinked out a few chords in different scales and felt his diving watch.

She asked how Terence was.

Andrei said that, "against all odds," Terence was teaching film at the local high school. He sat on the piano bench and asked whether she would pay in cash or by check.

She said she had no money and looked at her son, Tristan, tethered on the floor. He wrung his hands and quoted scripture in Latin. He was naked and hid the hair between his legs with his hands.

"How do you expect to pay?" asked Andrei. He looked closely at the photographs on the wall. There was a large photo of a boy with dull eyes taped to a photo of a woman he used to know who died in childbirth. He pretended not to stare at the photo of himself and Amelia. He smelled fish.

He felt the cracked music stand and asked if she wanted him to fix it.

She said he was the one who broke it all those years ago.

He coughed and unrolled his tools on the couch. Instead of tuning forks, wrenches, and mutes, Amelia saw a selection of knives ranging from small to very large. She stumbled backward into a tall empty dish cabinet. Tristan struggled to stand. He had read the manuscript in the piano and knew what was about to happen.

Eye for an Eye

After six weeks in high school, Tristan dislodged his chemistry partner's left eye. It was an accident, and avoiding Charlotte afterward became a full-time job. Much to Tristan's horror, they went to the same college. Charlotte wore wide hair bands that swept back her red hair in a puffy wave. A peace-sign patch covered her empty eye socket. She sat two seats behind Tristan.

"Hey," said Charlotte.

"Hey," said Tristan.

Tristan had beautiful brown eyes, and his head perched out too far from his neck, making him seem tentative.

Charlotte winked and doodled a Cyrillic yat on her notebook. Both the yat and yus had been eliminated in Bulgaria during the orthographic reform of 1945. The professor walked in, and chairs scraped the floor.

"Good morning, folks," said the professor. He looked at an eraser in the eraser board tray.

Charlotte raised her hand. "I need a clear view if you're going to use the eraser board." She flipped up her eye patch, revealing a pink, gummy slit.

Tristan moved to the window side of the room, near the back.

"Good to go?" asked the professor.

"That's much better," said Charlotte.

Tristan's Bible Study group met on Wednesdays in the student center. Everyone knew about Charlotte and the accident. It was their idea to encourage her to join the group.

"Zdravei, Tristan," said Charlotte. A small cross painted on her eyelid twisted and moved when she blinked, and it sort of looked cool.

"Hey," said Tristan. "Everyone, this is Charlotte."

"Hey guys," she said, tugging on her strapless dress.

A round of enthusiastic greetings spared the group a minute or so of anxiety. The room was blue and comfortable with tables and soft chairs. There was soda, bags of chips, and an empty coffee maker.

"Tristan and I went to high school together," said Charlotte. A murmur of animated responses followed. "His mother used to tie him to a piano naked, and he caused me to lose my left eye."

Tristan nodded and looked down. The blue room went a little gray. The group's leader said it would be good to start with prayer.

At least once a week, Charlotte required Tristan to participate in a live video chat. She could tell when he was and wasn't looking at the screen.

"Hey, Tristan," said Charlotte.

"Hey," said Tristan. He waited for the ordeal

to begin. His roommate, from Mount Athos in Greece, was at the rec center. His roommate's sister, who hailed from Macedonia, was also an incoming freshman. Charlotte's head filled his laptop screen.

Charlotte focused the gooseneck lamp on her face. With her fingers, she spread the lids apart. A pink wet muscle. She poked her finger in there. She looked at the objects in her lap. She picked up a pocketknife and slid it in, wincing.

Tristan closed his eyes.

"Open your eyes," said Charlotte.

His roommate, who had been kicked out of a monastery for forging incunabula, walked in, turned around, and left.

She stuck a thermometer in there.

Tristan graduated with his BA in film, Charlotte with a BS in philology and a minor in film. She was surprised when Tristan married and skipped graduate school. What the hell could he do with a bachelor's in film?

Tristan moved back to his hometown with his new Macedonian wife, Natalya, who was as thin and awkward as he was. She'd studied film as well. He was working at his old high school—a position had opened up—and Natalya was pregnant.

Against his better wishes, Natalya befriended Charlotte and even learned to push Charlotte's prosthetic eye in and out with her index finger.

It wasn't long before Charlotte was coming

over and sitting on the couch watching TV, next to
the aquarium filled with meaty silver fish. Natalya
made scraping noises in the kitchen, cooking a stew,
frying potatoes.

"Hey, Tristan," said Charlotte. She adjusted her
strapless dress and uncrossed her legs.

"Hey," said Tristan. He walked into the kitch-
en and kissed Natalya. She was very large and due
within the month.

Charlotte massaged the area over Natalya's uterus
to ease the cramps. Natalya relaxed on the bed and
fell into a troubled sleep. In the bright blue baby
room, Charlotte changed Henry's tiny diaper and
went to the kitchen for a grapefruit spoon.

When Tristan came home, Charlotte met him
in the doorway. He noticed her awful brown eye,
then looked at the green one, then back to the
brown one. He heard little Henry screaming and
Natalya shouting in her native tongue.

"Goodbye, Tristan," said Charlotte.

The Codex Marianus

Tristan heard a door open, a clumsy banging. In front of him, a Latin translation of a folio from the Codex Marianus lay on top of a small stainless steel wastebasket. The ancient text was penned in the Glagolitic alphabet, a precursor to Cyrillic. He glanced through the cracked bathroom door and saw a thin slice of mirror.

He heard a footstep or two in the bedroom. The manuscript spoke of a bleeding woman who tied her son to an enchanted harp. The window above him framed a square of that day. The sky was blue at the top, fading to a dull white at the bottom. He looked through the crack in the door and saw a sleeve in the mirror.

Out of courtesy, he flushed. The sleeve in the mirror did not move. "It's all my fault," said Tristan, hunched over the manuscript. The text spoke of a curse and the blinding of an evil man's grandson.

The man standing in the hall held an expensive chef's knife in his left hand. He squinted into the mirror and watched the man on the toilet. His curved spine seemed like knuckles beneath a film of rubber. "What you reading?" he said to the man on the toilet. He saw the man turn a page.

"An improbable tale," said Tristan. The paragraph at hand spoke of a thousand years of unholy

revenge. He raised the manuscript from the waste
bin with both hands. From the folio clung a damp
bandage, dangling by its adhesive strip.

The man in the hall laughed. "Guess what hap-
pens next?" A concertina in its case began to play.
A phonograph needle zipped across a vinyl record.
His heart fluttered, and his vision blurred. The man
on the toilet slumped as a knife went through the
rubber of his back.

When his wife discovered the body of a stranger
on the toilet, she discovered a manuscript written in
a strange but familiar alphabet. She roughly trans-
lated a parable that told of a "bullet" [an arrow]
that pierced a man, nicked a "piano," [an enchanted
harp] pierced a young woman, and lodged in anoth-
er. She hid the manuscript from the police and gave
it to her husband, Henry. He'd married her despite
the hydrocephalic child and wrote what years later
would in hindsight be described as slipped-disk
fiction.

As the universe began to recede, Tristan pulled
the bandage from the book's jacket and dropped it
into the bin. He looked through the crack in the
door and, in the mirror, saw a man who could very
well be his brother.

As the universe stuttered and resumed its
expansion, the door opened, and a man in a long-
sleeve shirt stood there with a knife. "It's time to
put the propaganda away," the man said.

"You're impossible," said Tristan, returning to

the first page. He read aloud the epigraph, penned
in Latin: "Revenge is mine."

"Them's not your words," said the man in the
coat. He pulled a piece of paper from his pocket.
"Them's the words of our grandfather Ilyich Lilov,
grandson of Marin Drinov, the famous philologist
and advocate of the 32-letter Cyrillic alphabet used
in Bulgaria until the orthographic reform of 1945,
which reduced the alphabet to 30 letters."

"Yes, Lilov was a staunch defender of his grandfather and the yat and yus. He was distinguished
by a long neck that made him seem tentative," said
Tristan. He turned the page.

A Thousand Years of Unholy Revenge

On Tuesday, Mario worried the fish was dead. He'd roughed up his girlfriend, Gina, the night before. If the fish died, it would be his fault, and his old lady, Gina, would have one up on him. He called the restaurant and got the answering machine.

Beep. "This is Mario, and the fish cannot die. You get me? Check on that damn fish. I'll go ahead and say the please word." Beep. He hung up the phone.

The day before, a man named Tristan had come by the restaurant, who regretted not trying to find his son after he had been whisked away to a monastery in Greece, where Bulgarian was widely spoken. This man had limped in during the lunch rush and told Mario he had a fish. Hmm, the restaurant's owner, having spent his youth in a monastery by the sea, had said something a few weeks back about fresh fish, so Mario took a look. The fish was as big as his thigh and breathing. It squirmed in a foam cooler slopping with mucky water, its thick tail thing bent double. A square head with bulbous eyes stuck out of the water, and it breathed like it was chewing. "What's that? Hair?" asked Mario. The hair reminded him of his boss's one-eyed wife.

Standing by the truck, this guy, Tristan, dropped his stabbing knife casually and asked Mario why he beat on his old lady so bad. It looked to Mario like a good day to buy fish. Eight bucks.

"Who you calling?" Gina stood stock-still in her bra and no underwear. Her green eyes blazed with premature triumph. "That fish die on you?"

Mario looked at her saggy bottom, the dollar bill–green prison tattoos, and the bruises on her waist. "Put your pants on," he said, listening for the neighbor's shower.

"Who you calling?" With her cane, Gina followed him into the bathroom, rust stains everywhere. She worked nights at the nursing home, answering the phone. On his nights off, sometimes Mario went with her to sample the medications and help out.

"I get some minutes and you on me about who's calling." Mario turned on the shower and held his splotched hand under the cold water. The pipes squealed like an infant born without a brain and a tail instead of legs.

"I hope your balls dry up," said Gina in Bulgarian. She left, thinly scratched her bottom, and threw back the wrinkled sheets. Sometimes the Bulgarian came back, whether she wanted it to or not. She crawled dead tired into the bed, smelled Mario in the mattress, and fell asleep.

The man named Tristan pulled his truck up to the nursing home. He cut the switch, and the engine rattled for a few seconds. He licked a sardine tin, brushed some cracker crumbs off his face, and limped on inside to visit with Lurla, his adopted daughter.

The visiting room up front was empty except for the wrinkled lady in yellow house shoes. She gazed longingly at him, like she might know him. "You smell like fish," she said as he passed.

"Yes, ma'am," said Tristan, removing his dirty hat. Several lights were out in the dim hall, which smelled like cat pee and mustard. The nursing station in the middle looked dead.

"Hi there, Mr. Tristan," said the short, fat nurse, Debbie Dee.

"Lo, Miss Debbie," said Tristan. He held his hat in his hands at waist level.

"She's back there, cuttin' up like usual." Rifling through charts and scribbling nonsense, Debbie Dee smiled a quick one, showing her sugar-rotted front teeth.

"Yes, ma'am." Tristan ran his fingers along the wall and walked on back there.

Lurla hung over sideways, strapped in the wheelchair. Her thick, foamy tongue poked in and out like an iguana's. Her eyes wobbled in her gi-ant translucent head. Her wadded gown showed a bloody diaper. Tristan walked over and straightened her as best he could. He could hear her heart mur-

mur from three feet off and saw it rippling across
her scalp.

"Lurla, you home?" The wheelchair rolled, and
he locked the wheels. Lurla made a vacuum cleaner
noise and balled her fists tight to her face.

Tristan picked up a soft brush. He arranged
Lurla's wispy red hair to hide the bald spot, fondled
her breast, and looked around for a clean diaper as
a thousand years of unholy revenge entered into the
past.

www.ingramcontent.com/pod-product-compliance
Lightning Source LLC
Chambersburg PA
CBHW042035180726
48295CB00006B/111